The Night I Helped Santa

The Night
I Helped
Santa

Gareth Baker

Illustrated by Vicky Kuhn

Published by Taralyn Books in October 2021
(Revised text and new art)
© Gareth Baker 2021
Art and Cover by Vicky Kuhn

ISBN: 9781694969705

For all the people who get excited about Santa.

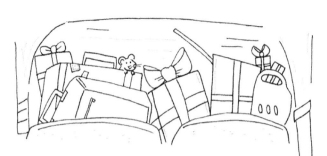

One

It was **Christmas Eve** and Karl

was on his way to his Granny's

house. He was very *excited*.

Karl and his family went to Granny's every Christmas, but this year it was going to be special. This year it wasn't just him, Mum and Tyrel who were going. It was also Cassie's first Christmas.

Cassie was Karl's baby sister. She was safely tucked into her car seat next to him.

"Mum," Karl said. "I can't see Teddy anywhere."

"It'll be okay. He'll be somewhere," Mum said.

Teddy was Cassie's favourite toy. She took him everywhere she went and would not sleep at night without him.

Karl had a good look around the back of the car. He looked on the seat. He looked on the floor. He looked everywhere. But he could not see **Teddy** anywhere.

'He's not here,' Karl said.

"Okay," said Tyrel. "Let's stop at this service station and have a good look. He has to be somewhere."

When they were parked, Karl looked in the car boot. It was full of suitcases, but there was no sign of **Teddy**.

"**Oh no,**" said Tyrel. "I've just remembered where **Teddy** is."

"Where is he?" asked Mum.

"I put him on the kitchen table so I wouldn't forget him and—" Tyrel stopped talking and covered his mouth.

"**You forgot him,**" Mum finished for him.

Tyrel nodded.

"Oh no. What are we going to do?" said Karl.

"We can't go back home. It's too far," Tyrel said.

"We will just have to hope that Cassie doesn't notice," said Mum.

Karl shook his head. "She'll notice as soon as she wakes up."

They walked to the main entrance of the service station and went inside.

"Mum?" Karl said, looking around. "Have we been here before?"

"Yes, we have. When Cassie was born, we came down to see Granny and we stopped here," she said.

"I knew it," Karl said. "This is where we bought **Teddy!** Maybe we could buy her a new one!"

Two

Karl pointed at a shop and said, "We got Teddy in there. Do you remember?"

"Oh, yes," Mum answered. "Why don't you and Tyrel see if you can find a new one while I feed Cassie?"

Karl and Tyrel made their way through the noisy crowds and into the shop. People were everywhere, picking up bottles of pop, sweets, colouring books and last-minute

Christmas cards.

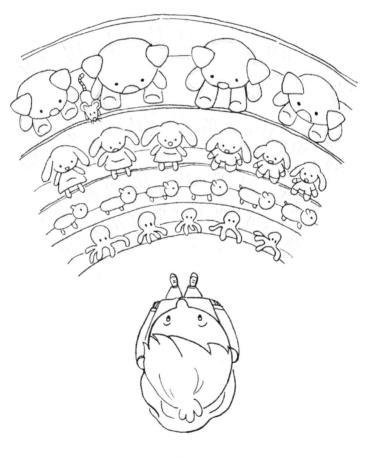

Karl found the toy section. There were pigs, **reindeer**, rabbits, **Santas**, sheep and **elves**. They had everything.

But there were no teddies.

Karl felt something bump into him. He turned around and saw a man carrying a big box.

"I'm sorry, sonny," came a deep voice.

Karl looked up, and his mouth fell open. The man had an enormous white beard and a shock of white hair on his head. He looked just like **Father Christmas**.

"Are you alright?" the man asked.

"Yes," Karl managed to say as he stared. "Do you work here?"

"Yes, I'm Chris," he said.

"I don't suppose you have any teddies," asked Tyrel.

"I don't know. I only work here at Christmas, but I could look in the back for you."

"Thank you so much," Karl said.

"Come back later," said Chris. "Hopefully, I'll have one for you."

Karl was just about to take Tyrel's hand and leave when he stopped and said, "Chris,

has anyone ever told you, you look like

Santa?"

"I get called **Father Christmas** *all* the

time," Chris laughed.

Karl and Tyrel left the shop and went and found Mum. Cassie had been fed and was fast asleep again.

"No luck?" said Mum.

Karl shook his head.

"We better get back on the road," said Tyrel.

They made their way through the crowds and went back to the shop.

There were still no teddies on the cuddly toy shelf. They went around and around the shop looking for Chris, but he was nowhere to be found.

"Excuse me, where's Chris?" Karl asked the man behind the till.

"No one called Chris works here," he said.

Three

It was warm in the car and Karl soon fell asleep. When he woke up again, they were at Granny's house. She lived in the countryside in an old **cottage**.

Granny's house was a really special place at **Christmas time**. The cottage was heated by log fires which meant **Father Christmas** could come down the **chimney**. She would

decorate it beautifully
and the smell of
delicious food filled
every room. Outside, she
would put **Christmas
lights** on the enormous
tree by her front gate. It
made it feel very
Christmassy and
magical.

Karl climbed out of the
car and jumped into his
Granny's waiting arms.

"Merry Christmas," she cheered.

"Merry Christmas, Granny."

"Come inside, it's cold out here," she said.

"I hope it snows tonight," Karl told her.

"That would be nice," Granny said. "Come on in, I've got some mince pies waiting."

Karl was not keen on mince pies, so he rushed up to his room. It was in the attic. It was the biggest room in the house! In the wall above the bed was a round window. Karl loved to look out at the countryside.

"This is where you're hiding," Granny said. She came into the room and sat down on the bed.

"I think I'm going to sit here all night and wait for **Santa** to come," Karl said.

"He won't come at all if you stay up," Granny warned.

"But I need to see him."

"Why?" asked Granny.

"Maybe **Santa** won't know we're here. Cassie's already lost **Teddy**. I don't want anything else to go wrong."

"Don't worry. **Santa** always knows where you are, even if you're visiting someone else."

Suddenly, Karl heard crying from downstairs. "**Oh no.** Cassie's woken up."

Four

Karl rushed downstairs. "What's

wrong?" he asked.

"Cassie's noticed **Teddy** is missing,"

explained Mum.

"Are you sure we can't go back and get him?" Karl asked.

"It's too far to go," Tyrel said.

"We would miss **Christmas** if we did," said Mum.

"I don't mind," Karl answered.

"You're a kind boy, Karl," said Granny. "It's time for our **Christmas Eve feast**."

Everyone cheered up. Granny's food was always delicious. There were sandwiches, cakes, salad and biscuits.

When everyone was full, they watched some television. Soon Karl started to **yawn**.

"I think you're tired," Tyrel said.

"Come on, Karl, it is bedtime," said Mum.

"I can't go yet. We still need to leave some treats out for **Santa and the reindeer**," Karl said.

"Come on then," smiled Granny.

Granny and Karl went into the kitchen and put a mince pie on a plate. Then they got a carrot and a saucer of milk for Rudolph. Finally, they poured a drink for Santa.

Karl put everything on a tray and put it by the fireplace in the living room.

He kissed everyone goodnight and went
to his room.

He put on his pyjamas and cleaned his
teeth. He jumped onto the bed and lay there
for a while.

But as hard as he tried, he could not fall asleep. He got up and looked out of the window above his bed.

"Amazing!" Karl said. He could not believe his eyes. The ground was sparkling in the moonlight. Everywhere was covered with snow!

Pure, white snow!

Then he heard something above him.

CRUNCH

CRUNCH

It was the sound of footsteps on snow,

and it was coming from the roof.

Karl looked up, his eyes wide with

excitement.

Someone was up there!

27

Five

Karl stared at the ceiling above him.

Footsteps.

On Christmas night.

It could only mean…

Remembering what Granny had said
about being awake when **Santa** came, Karl
buried himself down into his covers. If **Santa**

saw him, he would not leave any **presents**

and then *Cassie* would be even more upset.

CRUNCH

CRUNCH

Karl followed the sound of the footsteps

as they moved across the roof.

Where was **Santa** going?

Karl sat up in bed and looked at the opposite end of his bedroom where there was an empty fireplace. All the other fireplaces in Granny's cottage had a fire in them. This would be the only chimney in the whole house that Santa could use!

Karl was wondering what to do when...

A whole pile of snow fell down the chimney and into the fireplace.

Suddenly there came a frightened cry from up the chimney.

31

Karl threw back his covers and tiptoed across his carpet. He got down on his hands and knees and looked inside the fireplace.

"Look out below," cried a deep voice.

Karl jumped back, just as another mound of snow tumbled down the chimney.

"I'm sorry about that," came a chuckle from up the chimney.

"Santa? Is that you?" Karl asked.

"Who said I was Santa?" replied the voice.

"Who else would be climbing down a chimney on Christmas night?" Karl answered.

"I don't believe it," **Santa** said.

"You're not cross that I've guessed who you are, are you?" asked Karl.

"Not at all. I'm **stuck** in your chimney."

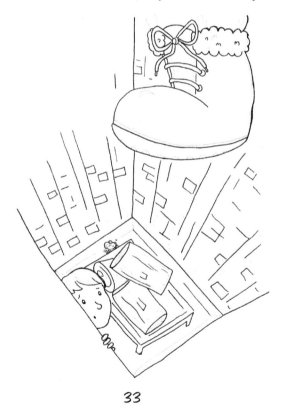

"Can I help?" Karl said, moving closer to the fire.

"Oh, yes, please. If I don't get a move on, I'm going to be running late. And if that happens, there will be lots of disappointed boys and girls."

"Hang on a minute," said Karl, "I need to turn the lights on so I can see what I'm doing."

"NO!" Santa cried. "Don't do that. You'll wake the grown-ups!"

"I might have a torch," suggested Karl.

"Don't worry. It is too late. I'm going to fall!" Santa cried.

Six

The chimney rumbled and a moment later snow poured all over the carpet. Then Santa came tumbling down and into Karl's bedroom.

He sat on the floor, a sack of presents behind him and a fur-edged hood draped over his face.

"Hello," said Karl.

"Hello," said Santa, pushing back his hood. He took off his glasses and cleaned them.

"How did you get on Granny's roof?" Karl asked.

"With my **reindeer**, of course. Thank goodness it snowed. It makes landing a lot easier when there is a nice, thick blanket of the white stuff."

"I'm sorry. I know I'm not supposed to see you," Karl said, suddenly feeling very worried. "Please give Cassie her **presents**, even if I can't have mine."

"Don't worry about it," **Santa** smiled.

"Are you sure?"

Santa nodded.

Karl smiled and helped Santa back onto his feet.

"I'm glad I've met you, Santa, because I really needed to speak to you," said Karl. "We accidentally left Cassie's **teddy** at home, and she needs a new one or she will spend the whole of **Christmas** crying."

"I see," said Santa, rubbing his thick, white beard.

"I'll give up all my **toys** if she can have a new **Teddy**."

"Would you really?" Santa said.

"Yes, I would. Cassie is the best baby sister I could ever have."

"Well," Santa began, "since you helped me out of the chimney, I should help you too."

"I didn't really help. You fell down by yourself," said Karl.

"Well, you tried to, that's what counts. I might have a spare teddy on my sleigh."

"Oh, thank you, thank you," Karl cried.

"There's only one tiny problem."

"What's that?" Karl asked.

"You would need to help me out a little bit more."

"What do you need me to do?" asked Karl.

"Well, first off we need to clear that mess up." Santa snapped his fingers and all the snow and soot disappeared from the carpet.

"**Wow**!" said Karl in amazement.

"Now to get back up on the roof," said Santa, pointing at the fireplace.

Karl looked at it nervously. "Is it hard climbing up there?"

Santa brushed a little bit of **soot** off his shoulder and said, "Don't worry, it's easy. Are you ready?"

"Will I need a coat?"

"My **sleigh** has its own heaters, the best the elves in my workshop can build. It's up to you."

Karl looked down at his pyjamas, but there was no time to waste.

"I'm ready."

Santa walked over to the chimney and stood next to it. "Ready?" he asked.

"Oh yes," Karl answered, barely able to contain his excitement.

Santa knocked on the chimney **three times.**

And ...

disappeared!

"Are you coming?" came Santa's voice from up the **chimney**.

"How?" asked Karl.

"Just knock on the wall three times."

Seven

Karl knocked on the chimney. One moment he was in his bedroom, the next he was sat in Santa's **sleigh**. Snow drifted through the night sky, but he was lovely and warm.

"This is **amazing**," Karl said.

Santa picked up the reins. He gave them a gentle flick and called, "**Rudolph**? Girls? We

have to get a move on. We're already late.
Let's go!"

The reindeer snorted and then started to
pull the sleigh across the snow-covered roof.

"It might be best if you sit down," Santa
said. "These guys can really…

flyyyyyy!"

The sleigh suddenly moved forward and
Karl was thrown back into his seat.

"I did warn you," Santa said with a
chuckle.

"It's okay," Karl laughed. "This is **unbelievable!**"

"It is. And do you know what? I never get **bored** of travelling this way. Now, we better head off for the **big city**," Santa said.

He pulled on the reins and steered the **reindeer** up and around in a big loop, back the way they had come.

"How **high** are we?" Karl asked.

"Look, there's an **aeroplane**. Shall we go and say hello?" said Santa, pointing.

"But what if someone sees us?" **Santa** smiled.

"Oh," said Karl.

"Besides, only people who **believe** in

me can see us."

"Really?"

"Yes. It's all done with **elf magic**. My helpers are amazing. Everyone should thank them really, not me."

"Elf magic? Is that how we got up the chimney?"

"Exactly," said Santa. "Come on. Let's go and see the plane."

Santa pulled on the reins and the team of **reindeer** gently swooped up. They climbed higher and higher into the swirling **snow** and sparkling stars. Santa skilfully flew them over to the plane.

Karl looked at a window and saw a little girl staring back at him.

Eight

Karl waved at the little girl, and she waved back. Her eyes were as big as saucers. Karl was not sure who was more surprised. Him or her.

"Can we get closer?" Karl asked.

"My reindeer can do anything," Santa laughed.

Santa pulled on the reins and the sleigh moved

nearer to the side of the plane. They

were *really* close. Karl reached over the side and put his hand on the window.

The girl put her hand up too and they **smiled** at each other.

"Come on. We'd better go," **Santa** said, and they started to move away.

Karl waved at the girl and gave her the biggest smile in the world. "I can't find the words to describe how **amazing** this is," he said.

"I'm glad you're enjoying it because now the **work** begins."

"What do I need to do?" Karl asked, barely holding in his excitement.

"Oh, only deliver everyone's **presents**."

Karl looked over his shoulder at the enormous pile of **sacks** behind him. When he looked back over the front of the **sleigh**, he could see hundreds and hundreds of sparkling lights.

It was the **big city**.

"Have we got to deliver to all of those houses?" he asked. It looked impossible.

"We don't have to do them all. If you help me deliver just some of the presents, we'll have enough time to go for another trip before I take you home."

"Of course, I'll help. I **wish** tonight could last forever," Karl said.

Santa smiled. "Right, hold on tight and I'll take us down."

The **sleigh** tipped to the left and they swooped down through the sky. The lights far below grew brighter and brighter as they got closer and closer.

"There are so many lights," Karl said.

"And so many children," Santa agreed. "If you lift up your seat, you'll find my spare suit. Pop it over your clothes. There should be some boots, too."

"But it'll be too big, unless, let me guess, elf magic makes it fit everyone?"

"You've got it," Santa laughed.

Karl put on the suit. It fitted him perfectly. And so did the shiny, black boots.

"How do I look?" Karl asked.

"To use one of your words —

amazing!"

"Where do we start?" Karl asked.

"Those flats over there," Santa said, pointing over the side of the sleigh.

Karl quickly counted how many floors there were.

"There must be lots of children in there."

"One hundred and twenty-three," Santa said.

"How do you remember that?" asked Karl, amazed at Santa's memory.

Santa tapped the side of his head. "I'm Santa, I remember everything. And just in case I do forget…" Santa reached inside his

coat, pulled out a folded piece of paper.

"What's this?"

"Open it and find out," said Santa.

Nine

Karl opened the
letter. He could not
believe it. It was
the one he had
written to Santa a
few months ago. It
was a list of things
he would like for **Christmas**.

It also told **Santa** about his little sister and how much he loved her.

"You got it," Karl gasped.

"Of course, I did," Santa said. "Now, let's get these presents delivered."

"But the block of flats doesn't have a **chimney**," Karl said. "How will we drop them off?"

"Don't worry about that," Santa said. "If I deliver to a house and it doesn't have a chimney, I have a **magic key**. If it's a flat, the elves and I have come up with something really special. Right, prepare for landing."

Karl sat down and the **reindeer** curved through the air. They landed softly on the snow-covered roof and the **sleigh** glided to a gentle halt.

"Are you ready?" asked Santa.

'Oh yes,' answered Karl.

Santa looked through the pile of **sacks** on the back of the sleigh. "Here," he said, handing Karl a large sack bursting with **toys** and presents. "This is the one you'll need."

Karl sat and stared at it.

"It looks like it weighs a ton!" Karl said.

"Don't worry. **Elf magic** will make it as light as a feather," Santa said. "Now, you take this side of the tower block, and I'll take the other."

"But how do I get into each flat?"

"All you need to do is walk down the side of the building and go in through the window," said Santa.

"Walk?" Karl started to feel a little worried.

"Yes. Watch me do it first if you want. You'll be safe, I promise."

Karl followed Santa to the edge of the tall building.

"See you soon," Santa said.

He stepped over the side. Instead of falling, something amazing happened. He just stepped around the corner and onto the wall as if he had just walked around the corner of a street.

"Just believe and the **elves** will do the rest," Santa said. "But never do it unless I'm with you. Okay?"

"okay, Santa," promised Karl.

Santa began to walk down the wall towards the first window.

Karl walked over to his side of the tower block. He felt very nervous, but he trusted Santa. And the elves. He took a deep breath and closed his eyes. Then he took a step forward and said, "I believe in Santa."

He knew the magic had worked. He could feel it. His feet were stuck to the wall!

"Amazing!" he said and walked down until he came to the first window. He

stepped onto it and

something amazing

happened.

Sluuuuurp!

Karl passed straight

through the window like it

was made of jelly. When

he landed on the other

side, he was stood on the

floor in a bedroom.

"This elf magic is cool!"

he said, and quickly put his

hand over his mouth.

69

There was **snoring** coming from the corner of the room. Karl tip-toed across the carpet and past a sleeping child. Carefully, he opened the bedroom door and crept down the hallway to the other end.

Karl poked his head around the door frame. In the corner of the room was a big **Christmas tree**. He stepped into the room. Now the work really began.

Ten

Karl put the sack on the floor and looked inside it.

"How am I supposed to know which ones to leave?" Karl said.

He reached into the sack and his hand was pulled towards a present wrapped in pink paper.

"It must be more elf magic,"

Karl whispered.

He quickly put the **present** under the tree and tip-toed back to the window.

He passed straight through the glass and back onto the outside of the tower block. Ten minutes later, Karl met **Santa** on the roof.

"You've done a good job. That's saved me loads of time. We'd better get you back home," Santa said.

"Okay," Karl said as he clambered up into the **sleigh**.

The **reindeer** pulled them along and soon they were back up in the sky.

"Hey! I recognise this street!" Karl said as they went lower. "That's my house!"

"We're not dropping off this time," said Santa. "We're picking up."

Eleven

Karl held onto the side of the sleigh as
Santa landed it on the soft snow on the roof
of his house.

"Why have we come all the way back
here?" Karl asked.
  "This is why I came to pick you up in the
first place. You've used the elf magic. Do

you really think I fell down your

chimney?" Santa took off his

hood and glasses.

Karl could not believe who was sitting in

front of him. It was the old

man from the newsagents with the kind,

sparkly eyes.

"You're **Chris!**" Karl cried.

The old man nodded and put his glasses and hood back on.

"Why didn't I recognise you before?" Karl asked. Santa smiled and Karl knew the answer.

"**Elf magic,**" they both said together.

"Some people call me **Father Christmas,** so when I am not doing this important job, I just call myself Chris."

"But it's **Christmas Eve.** This is your busiest day of the year. Why were you at a motorway service station?" asked Karl.

"Every year I find **special children** from all over the world," said Santa.

"I'm not **special**," said Karl.

Santa smiled. "And that's what makes you special, Karl. You were more worried about your baby sister than yourself. You are **kind** and **thoughtful**."

"But there must be other children that deserve your time more than me," said Karl.

"Maybe. It's true there are children who are **poorly**, and children who don't have all the lovely things you do, but **caring about others** is something I especially admire."

"I don't know what to say," Karl said.

"You don't need to say anything. Just promise me one thing."

"Anything, Santa."

"Always be kind to other people."

"I promise," Karl said, shaking Santa's hand.

"Right," Santa laughed, "Knock on that chimney pot, get **Teddy**, and let's get *you* back to Granny's."

Twelve

Karl woke up.

It was still dark inside his bedroom. He threw back his covers and turned to face the round window.

The glass was completely covered in snow and he could not see out.

Karl jumped out of bed and ran to the chimney. He knocked on the wall three times, but nothing happened.

Suddenly he realised he could not remember coming back to Granny's house. Had Santa used more elf magic? Or had it all been a dream?

Karl ran to Cassie's bedroom door.

"**Merry Christmas**, Cassie," Karl said as he walked into the room.

Cassie gurgled at him. She was trying to stand up in her cot. Karl peered over the edge. If he had helped Santa last night and got **Teddy,** surely, he would have put him in the cot with Cassie. Karl had a good look, but he could not see Teddy anywhere.

Karl felt sad. It *had* all been a dream.

"Merry Christmas!"

Karl turned around. Mum and Tyrel were stood in the bedroom door. He ran up to them and gave them a big hug.

"Happy Christmas," he shouted.

"Ggggh gh ghh gghhhh!"

Karl spun round.

"Did Cassie just say Merry Christmas?"

"Santa's been and it looks like he enjoyed the food we left," Mum said.

"Excuse me," Karl said. He quickly squeezed past them and ran down the stairs and into the kitchen.

"Merry Christmas!" Granny called as he burst through the door. "Santa left a note and an extra present for you. You'd better go and have a look."

Karl stared at the brightly wrapped gift and slowly walked over to it. He picked up the note, opened it and read it.

Without saying another word, Karl ran over to his **Granny** and hugged her. Then he went back upstairs with the present.

"What have you got there?" Mum asked.

"It's a present for Cassie," said Karl.

"That's so kind," said Mum. "When did you have a chance to get her one?"

Karl smiled. "I have special friends who helped me pick it up. Open it up."

"Why don't you open it for her," Mum said.

"Okay," said Karl.

They all sat on the floor and Karl slowly

unwrapped the paper and opened the box.

He felt so **excited**. Could it really be what he thought it was?

"It's a new **Teddy**," Mum said.

"No, it's not," said Tyrel, "It *is* Teddy. But I left him at home."

"How on earth did it get here?" Mum asked.

"That's the magic of Christmas," Karl said.

About the Author

Gareth loves Christmas, teddies and staying at Granny's. He hopes you've enjoyed the story. Make sure you get into bed nice and early on Christmas night!

Make sure you visit

gareth-baker.com

or try the following books

Wishes can come true

STAR FRIEND

Gareth Baker

MOGGY
ON A
MISSION

Gareth
Baker

Illustrated by Vicky Kuhn

Printed in Great Britain
by Amazon

76852486R00058